NEW FRIENDS FOR SAMMY

Written by Julie Monahan
Illustrated by Ann Wilson

Sammy the Flying Squirrel lived among the leaves and branches of the treetops in a large forest. Today was his first day of school and he was very excited.

At breakfast Sammy's mother told him what school would be like. "School is a place where you learn new things and make new friends."

"In school, you will meet many other kinds of animals," Mrs. Squirrel said. "Rabbits and frogs and beavers. Turtles and chipmunks and maybe skunks."

Sammy was a litttle scared. Until then, he had only known other squirrels. He had never even seen any of the other animals his mother was talking about.

Suddenly, he heard the school bus coming through the forest. "Honk! Honk!" It stopped at the bottom of Sammy's tree. He scampered down quickly.

"Welcome aboard!" said the bus driver.

The bus was full of little animals from all over the forest.

Sammy sat down next to another furry creature.

"What kind of animal are you?" he asked.

"Why, a chipmunk, of course," was the answer.
"My name is Chuck."

Sammy had never met a chipmunk before, but
Chuck was very friendly.

When they got to school, the teacher announced Show-and-Tell. One at a time all the animals went to the front of the classroom to show what made them different from the others.

First was the turtle. "This shell is where I live. It's hard on the outside, but warm and dry inside."

Next was the rabbit. "My long floppy ears tell me quickly if there is danger nearby."

Then it was Chuck's turn, Sammy's chipmunk friend.
"I use my cheeks to store and carry food until
I get back home."

Next was the frog, who stuck out his tongue!
"I like flies," he explained.
"I use my long tongue to catch them as they go by."

And then went the beaver.

"My tail is flat and wide. I can use it as a paddle to help me swim across the stream."

Then came the skunk.

"When someone comes by who gives me a fright,
I can spray a smell that will last all night!"

Then it was Sammy's turn. He didn't
say a word, but climbed proudly to the top of the
highest bookcase. Then he jumped off.

Sammy glided across the classroom and landed
softly on Chuck Chipmunk's desk.

The other little animals were not impressed.

"What's the good of knowing how to fly?" they asked. "Everything we need is on the ground. Our houses, our food, even the school. Flying is for the birds!"

Sammy felt very badly. He had always been
happy soaring and gliding in the treetops. On the bus
going home, he sat all by himself. He didn't want to
be a squirrel who could fly. He wanted to be just like
all the other little animals.

All of a sudden, the bus jumped and stopped,
landing in a muddy ditch.

"The bus is sinking!" the little animals cried as
they felt it go deeper and deeper into the thick mud.

Without a moment's delay, Sammy leaped out of his seat and out of the bus. He flew up to the treetops, gliding from branch to branch.

He never stopped until he reached the forest rescue team. "Help! Help!" he shouted. "The school bus is sinking!"

Sammy led the rescuers to the bus. It was almost
completely sunk in the thick gooey mud.

"Hurry, hurry!" cried the frightened little animals inside.

The rescue animals put heavy ropes under the bus, and heaved and pulled with all their might. At last the bus was on safe ground again.

All the little animals came running off the bus, yelling and cheering.

"Hurray for Sammy! Hurray for Sammy the Flying Squirrel!"

Sammy was proud and happy as the other little animals gathered around him. Now he felt like one of them. In some ways, each of them was different. But happy and safe together, they were all the same.